Written by Leigh Olsen. Based on the story "The Charming Gift," written by Ellie O'Ryan.
Illustrated by Elisabetta Melaranci, Chun Liu, and Gabriella Matta.

For information address Disney Press,
1101 Flower Street, Glendale, California 91201.

Printed in China
First Edition
1 3 5 7 9 10 8 6 4 2
ISBN 978-1-4847-0280-2
T425-2382-5-13338

For more Disney Press fun, visit www.disneybooks.com
This book was printed on paper created from a sustainable source.

Belle and the Charming Gift

Disney PRESS

New York • Los Angeles

Belle was reading a book in the library when she heard a loud crash! A tree branch had fallen through the window behind her. Papers were blowing all over the room.

Picking up the papers, Belle found one that looked especially interesting.

"What's this?" she asked Mrs. Potts.

"Why, that's an invitation to our annual ball," said Mrs. Potts. "We used to have it every year. Before . . ."

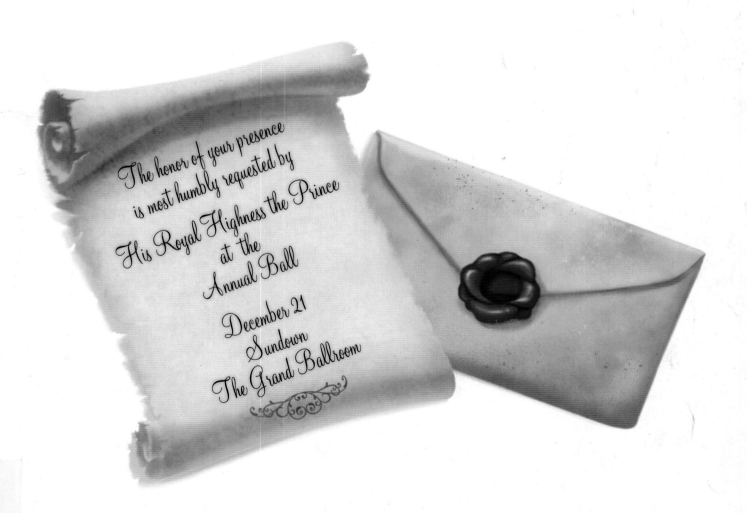

The honor of your presence
is most humbly requested by
His Royal Highness the Prince
at the
Annual Ball

December 21
Sundown
The Grand Ballroom

Belle was excited. She had never
been to a ball.

Finding the Beast, she showed him
the invitation. "Wouldn't it be lovely to
have another ball?" she asked.

The Beast thought for a moment. He saw how excited Belle was and didn't want to disappoint her. "Very well," he agreed. "But only for those of us inside the castle."

"Oh, thank you!" cried Belle. "You won't be sorry!"

And with that, the enchanted objects set off to get the castle ready for the ball.

While Cogsworth prepared the ballroom, Mrs. Potts and the Wardrobe helped Belle choose a new gown.

"Oh, this is perfect!" Belle cried.

But the Wardrobe was not finished. "Now for my favorite part," she said. "Accessories!"

The Wardrobe's drawers flew open to reveal trays of sparkling jewels.

Belle oohed and aahed over the jewels. Then, suddenly, she grew sad.

"What is it, dear?" asked Mrs. Potts.

"These are all beautiful. I just wish I had my charm bracelet. My father made it for me. It had five tiny charms on it: a rose, a teacup, a sprig of holly, a star, and a snowflake."

Mrs. Potts could tell Belle was homesick. Luckily, she had an idea.

Mrs. Potts gathered the Beast, Chip, Cogsworth, and Lumiere. She told them about the charm bracelet Belle's father had made her.

"We can't give Belle her old bracelet, but what if we make her a new one?" she asked.

The Beast thought that was a wonderful idea and led the objects to the royal jewelry chamber.

"Everyone gather the jewels you need," said Mrs. Potts. "Have your charm ready before the ball begins!"

Mrs. Potts and Chip gathered their jewels and headed to the kitchen. They had just laid everything out when Belle appeared.

Quick as a flash, Chip leaped into the air, flipped, and landed upside down . . . right over the jewels!

"Don't mind me. I'm just getting a snack!" Belle said, grabbing a scone.

As soon as she left, Chip and Mrs. Potts got to work. They cut a teacup shape out of tin and glued their jewels on top.

It was perfect!

Happy with the teacup charm, Chip headed to the study to help Lumiere. On his way there, he ran into Belle. She was going to the study, too!

"I just finished filling the ballroom with flowers," Belle told Chip. "I thought I'd put the extras in the study."

"Why don't I take those for you," Chip said. "I'm going that way."

"Oh, would you?" Belle said. "Now I can go back to decorating the ballroom!" And with that, she hurried off in the opposite direction.

Inside the study, Chip found Lumiere covered in glue!

"What happened?" asked Chip.

Lumiere sighed. "I was trying to glue these gold flakes to a piece of paper, but the glue is too gooey. And now I have made a mess!"

"Hmmm," said Chip. "What if we use candle wax?"

Chip helped Lumiere shape some wax into a star. Then he dusted the star with gold flakes.

The charm gleamed like a real star!

Chip left the study and found Cogsworth in the greenhouse.

"What are you doing in here?" asked Chip.

"I am making a holly charm for Belle," said Cogsworth. "Only, I don't know what holly looks like. I came here to find some, but there isn't any!"

"There's a holly bush outside, next to the fountain," said Chip. "I'll ask the Beast if he can get some for you."

   The Beast agreed and was just putting on his coat as Belle came into the hall.

   "Where are you going?" she asked the Beast.

   "I, uh, need to get some holly for Cogsworth to decorate with," the Beast said nervously.

   "I'll come with you!" said Belle.

Finally, the Beast came back inside with holly sprigs for Cogsworth.

"Splendid!" Cogsworth said, and he got to work. "Now I just need two rubies for the berries," he continued a short time later.

But as Chip bounced over with a bag of jewels, he tripped. The jewels scattered all over the greenhouse.

"Oh, no!" Chip cried. He was sure the Beast would be furious.

But the Beast just smiled and said, "It's okay, Chip. I'm done with my charm. I'll find the jewels and you can help Cogsworth finish his charm."

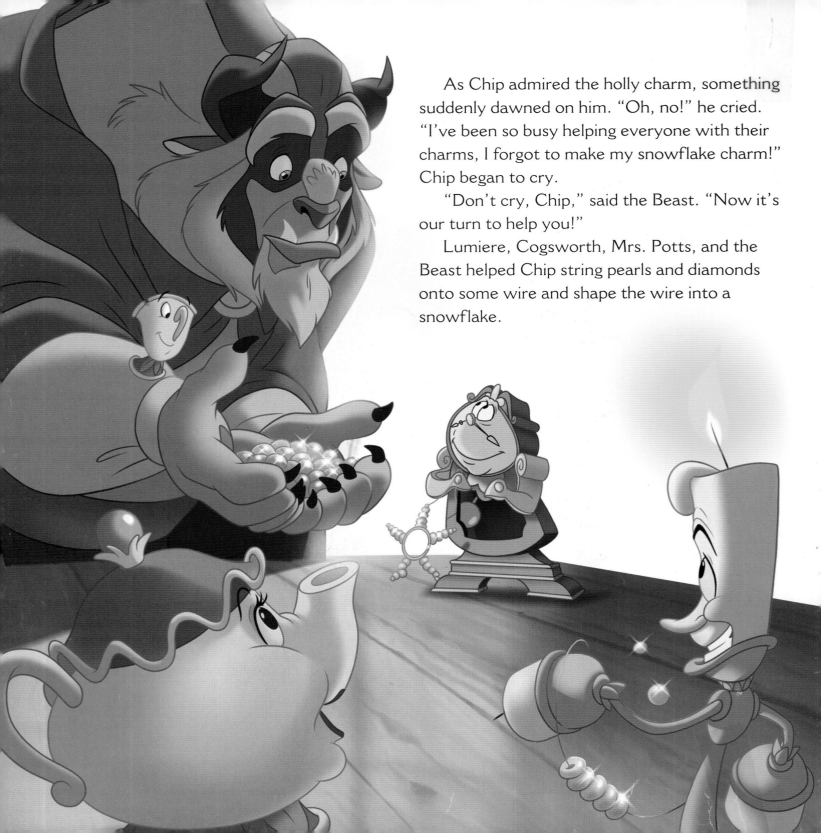

As Chip admired the holly charm, something suddenly dawned on him. "Oh, no!" he cried. "I've been so busy helping everyone with their charms, I forgot to make my snowflake charm!" Chip began to cry.

"Don't cry, Chip," said the Beast. "Now it's our turn to help you!"

Lumiere, Cogsworth, Mrs. Potts, and the Beast helped Chip string pearls and diamonds onto some wire and shape the wire into a snowflake.

The Beast put all the charms on a gold bracelet.

"Chip," said Mrs. Potts, "I think you should present the bracelet to Belle. After all, you helped make all the charms!"

The Beast nodded and dropped the charm bracelet into the little teacup. "Now, let's hurry, everyone," he said. "The ball is about to begin!"

While the other enchanted objects helped the Beast get dressed, Mrs. Potts headed to Belle's room to help her get ready. She could see that the girl was still sad.

Suddenly there was a knock on Belle's door.

Belle opened the door and Chip hopped inside.

"Why, what do we have here?" Belle asked curiously as Chip spilled the bracelet into her open palm.

Belle gasped. "A charm bracelet? For me?"

Tears sprung to Belle's eyes as she looked at the bracelet.

"When we heard about the bracelet your father gave you, we thought you should have one to wear tonight," Mrs. Potts said.

"We hope you like it," the Beast said, poking his head into Belle's room along with Lumiere and Cogsworth.

"It's beautiful," said Belle. "It's not the same as my old one, but that doesn't make it any less special. Thank you. Thank you all. I love my bracelet so much. I can't wait to wear it tonight!"

And that is just what she did. As the enchanted
objects watched, Belle and the Beast waltzed
through the room. Belle's charm bracelet caught
the light whenever she moved.

Chip couldn't help but smile. It was the perfect
party.